I would like to dedicate this book to my grandfather, Abbas Kheiriyeh, who was a rug weaver in the city of Kashan, Iran.

Reycraft Books
55 Fifth Avenue
New York, NY 10003
Reycraftbooks.com

Reycraft Books is a trade imprint and trademark of Newmark Learning, LLC.

Educators and Librarians: Our books may be purchased in bulk for promotional, educational, or business use. Please contact sales@reycraftbooks.com.

Library of Congress Cataloging-in-Publication Data is available.

ISBN: 978-1-4788-6907-8
Author photo courtesy of Rashin Kheiriyeh.
Printed in Guangzhou, China.
4401/1119/CA21902021
10 9 8 7 6 5 4 3 2 1
First Edition Hardcover published by Reycraft Books.

Reycraft Books and Newmark Learning, LLC, support diversity and the First Amendment, and celebrate the right to read.

REYCRAFT
BOOKS

Bahar, the Lucky

written and illustrated
by Rashin Kheiriyeh

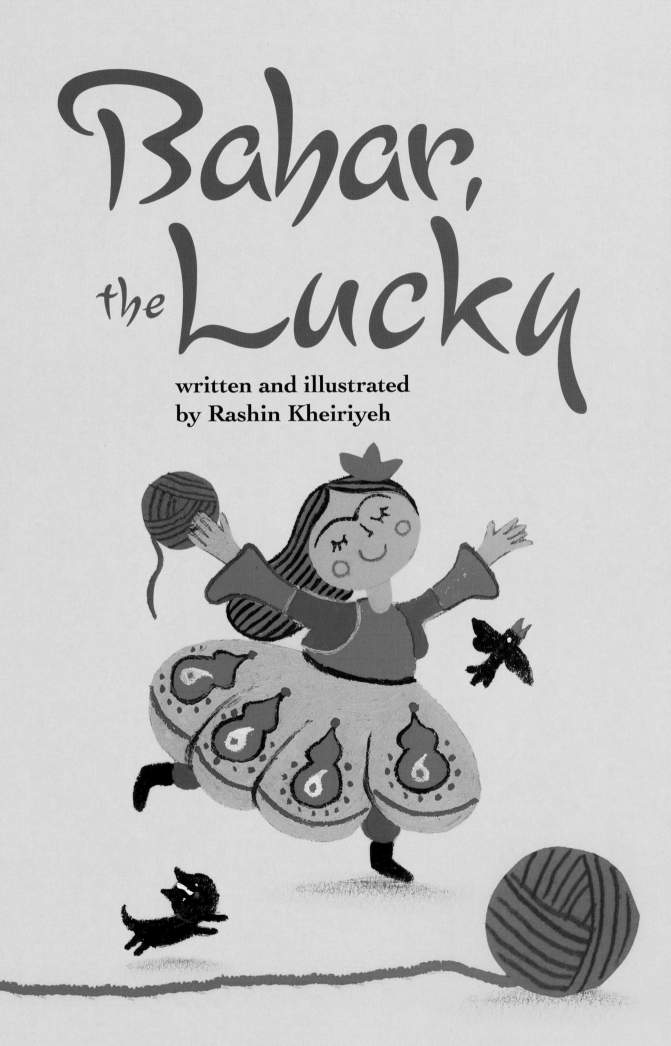

L ong ago
in the Grand Bazaar of Kashan,
there was a young girl who was
a rug weaver. Her name was Bahar and
she had learned to weave rugs from her
grandmother. The rugs had the most
beautiful patterns in all the city.

For each rug she sold, Bahar only earned
a few coins. Her mother depended on
these to pay for the wheat and milk her
children needed.

It was all they had to eat.
Even so, they felt blessed
in their hearts.

The trouble began on the day Bahar went to the town's hammam to shower. The public bath had been reserved for the wife of the king's chief fortune teller and no one was allowed to enter.

"It has been so long since I was last here," begged Bahar. "Please let me bathe in the corner with the maids." The bath owner agreed, but warned her to be careful.

"The chief fortune teller's wife must not notice you are here," he said.

Soon after, the fortune teller's wife walked in, proud as a camel.

Bahar, lost in imagining herself wrapped in the riches of a fortune teller, tripped over a stool and fell into the pool.

Everyone laughed.

Except the chief fortune teller's wife.

Bahar leapt up and ran home, followed by the shouts of the angry bath owner.

Bahar's mother sat her next to the fire to warm her. That evening, everyone spoke about the riches of the chief fortune teller and his wife.

"My days as a rug weaver are over,"

proclaimed Bahar as she stood. "I too can be a fortune teller.
As good as the chief fortune teller. And I will rescue us from poverty."

The following day, Bahar quit selling her rugs and bought the tools for fortune telling. A small round tray. A metal goblet adorned with stars. And three dice bearing strange signs. She then sat on a street corner.

Soon, two of the king's servants came running. "Oh master of mysteries, tell us where we can find the king's cat. The silkiest and fluffiest of all Persians has disappeared. If you don't help us find it, the king will chop us into a hundred pieces.

And you with us!"

Terrified, Bahar threw the dice. She then reached into
her pouch for a handful of pistachios.

"Here. Walk straight ahead. As you do, each of you
will eat one pistachio, then another, and another,
and so on. When you are out of pistachios,
turn around four times. Then take forty steps
and you will find the cat. Make sure you
make no mistakes."

The two servants took the pistachios
and began walking.

But Bahar feared they
would never find the king's cat.

So, after eating the last pistachio, the palace servants turned around four times and walked forty steps.

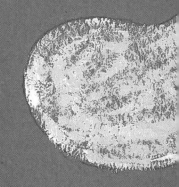

In front of them crouched the cat drinking from the fountain in the main town square.

The two servants burst with joy. With the silkiest and fluffiest Persian in their arms, they ran back to Bahar to give her ten gold coins as a reward. Bahar couldn't understand any of this, but she thanked Heaven.

Returning home,
her family congratulated her.

Early the next morning, Bahar headed back to the same street corner to set up her box. The mayor was waiting. "Are you the town's new fortune teller everyone is talking about?" he asked.

Bahar had no time to be afraid or to answer.

"In that case," he said, "it should be easy for you to find where the forty thieves hid the king's crown, designed with diamonds and precious gems. If you don't," added the mayor, "he'll hang the both of us."

"I'll give you my answer tomorrow," said Bahar.

The mayor gave her a generous advance of a hundred gold coins.

Back home, Bahar's mother cooked a delicious meal to celebrate their good fortune. But Bahar couldn't eat. She had no idea how to find the crown and wondered how she would get out of this alive.

Bahar went to her room to finish a rug she was weaving for her mother's birthday. It had a beautiful image of a pomegranate tree. She missed the peace and safety of weaving her rugs.

Suddenly, she heard whispers.

Two of the forty thieves peeked through the window.

They came in and bowed humbly before her. "Oh great master of fortune telling, obviously you have discovered that we hid the king's crown under the biggest tree in the pomegranate garden," the thieves said, pointing to the rug's pattern. "All we ask is that you not reveal our forty faces to the king. Here are one hundred gold coins to thank you in advance for your kindness."

They gave Bahar the bag
of gold coins and snuck away.

The next morning, Bahar led the mayor to the pomegranate garden. Together, they dug under the biggest tree and found the crown.

Eager to save himself, the mayor raced back to the king, forgetting to ask the identity of the thieves.

That very afternoon, the king summoned Bahar to the palace. He showered her with gifts to thank her, while musicians played and dancers swirled about her. All under the jealous eyes of the chief fortune teller and his wife.

A girl like this could never be a real fortune teller," the chief fortune teller said to the king. "Give her one more test and I will prove she is a fake."

He shot Bahar a wicked smile, then hid a cricket in his hand.

"My majesty, if this so-called fortune teller is real, she will tell us what I have in my fist," he said.

Bahar cursed herself for starting this dangerous fortune telling game. She closed her eyes in search of a bright answer within the darkness of her thoughts. An old Iranian proverb appeared and slipped through her lips.

Once, you bounce the cricket,

Twice, you bounce the cricket,

At last, you are caught in the hand, cricket!

"Bravo!" the king said. He then opened the chief fortune teller's fist as the cricket jumped out. The king immediately fired his fortune teller and declared Bahar as his chief fortune teller for life.

As soon as the king's words echoed through the palace's
Great Hall, Bahar dashed into the crowd.

And disappeared.

To this day, no one has ever spotted the
lucky girl again. But every now and then
a rug with the most beautiful patterns
appears in the Grand Bazaar of Kashan.